Edd's Ghost Story

Christina Mackay-Robinson

Illustrated by Paul Johnson

BBC BOOKS

"Do I *have* to stay with Aunt Vera?" Edd complained. "She's so bossy and she's always telling me off."

"Now, don't be rude, Edd," said Mum as they sped along in the taxi. "Just think, this may be your last chance to play in her lovely big garden."

   Aunt Vera had a huge old house called Mallard Manor
but it stood in the way of plans for a new motorway.
Edd's mum had to find her a new home urgently – but the
thought of house-hunting with Edd was . . . well . . . first
he'd get bored, then he'd get up to no good. So she decided
that Edd should stay with his aunt while she looked for a
new home.

The taxi pulled up outside Mallard Manor. Edd noticed the curtains twitch.

"Probably saw us five miles away with her big nose," he thought, slouching through the gate.

"Stop dragging your feet, Edd!" hissed his mother.

Aunt Vera bustled along the garden path.

"Yes, young man, we'll have none of that!" She bent down and offered him a feathery cheek.

"First she tells me off and then she expects a kiss! Well, tough!!" He duck-dived past her up the path. Edd's mum led him firmly up the steps. He was in for a lecture.

"You must be polite to your auntie. How would you feel if your house was to be demolished?"

"Hope she'll be in it," mumbled Edd.

As he spoke he had a strange feeling that someone was watching them. He was so absorbed in his thoughts that he hardly felt his mother slap his legs.

Before long Edd's mum had left. He sat miserably in his bedroom.

"Tea's ready!" shouted Aunt Vera.

As he made his way down the oak staircase Edd noticed that the tenth step creaked. He knew the noise would irritate his aunt so he jumped up and down on it.

"RIGHT, that's enough!" yelled his aunt. "No tea for you. And I'd made you a chocolate sponge. Go straight back to your room."

"It's not fair!" pleaded Edd.

"It's time you learnt your lesson," said his aunt. "And stop dragging your feet. I won't tell you again."

"What a spooky house," thought Edd, his tummy
rumbling as he trudged back upstairs.
   Suddenly he had a wicked idea. He ran into his room,
grabbed the sheet from his bed and tossed it over his head.
   "This'll frighten the old stinky."

Edd crept down the stairs in his ghost outfit and sneaked behind the sofa.

"Wooa . . . Wooa . . ." he moaned.

"W . . . What's that?" Aunt Vera gasped, catching her breath.

Edd jumped out, wailing.

"*Aaaagh!!!*" Aunt Vera leapt to her feet, whipping the sheet from his head and stood towering above him. It was Edd's turn to be frightened. Aunt Vera dragged him by the mohican all the way back to his room. But instead of telling him off, she began sobbing.

Edd felt dreadful. "I'm sorry . . ." he stammered. Aunt Vera dabbed the tears from her eyes. "I'll behave from now on," said Edd.

"I do hope so. The nice man from the Council is coming tomorrow. It's my last chance to change his mind about the house, so I want you on your best behaviour."

Edd promised, but then things always seemed to go wrong with Edd's promises . . .

That night as he lay in bed, Edd heard a low moaning.
"Oh dear, Aunt Vera must still be upset," he thought.
But the noise was coming from somewhere in his room.
Suddenly through the wall came a ghost – a *real* ghost!

"Eeeeedddddd theeeee duuuuuck . . . I have come to geeeet youuuuu!"

Edd quacked loudly with terror. He dived under the bedclothes, but a pair of cold hands wrenched the quilt from him. They belonged to his aunt.

"Edd, are you having a bad dream?" Aunt Vera looked worried.

"The g . . . g . . . ghost . . ." he stammered.

"Oh, stuff and nonsense," she said crossly. "And you promised you were going to behave."

"There really was a ghost, Auntie."

Aunt Vera did her best to calm her nephew before finally leaving the room.

He had just convinced himself that it had been in his imagination when a cheeky voice said, "What d'ya wanna go and do that for?"

Edd slowly sat up in bed. The ghost was back, perched on the top of the wardrobe.

"W . . . W . . . Who are you?" Edd stuttered.

"I've been watchin' your antics. Decided to give ya a bit of your own medicine," he said, "but ya didn't need to call in the ol' dear."

Edd was bewildered.

"Ya can't go tellin' grown-ups about us ghosts." Suddenly the spirit laughed. "Coo – didn't 'alf scare ya – ya big chicken!"

"Chicken! I'm a duck!" Edd was offended. "Me? Scared? Never! So, then, are you a real ghost?" he added, trying to be cool.

"Course I am, ya stoopid duck."

"Well, what's your name, spooky dude?" Edd snapped.

"Frank."

"Frank the Ghost! Very frightening – I DON'T think," Edd sniggered.

"What's so funny, big beak?" Then Frank suddenly turned serious. "Look, Edd, I need your help. I've lived in this house for 332 years and I ain't leavin'! What's this about a Council bloke comin' round 'ere?"

"He wants Auntie to sign the papers so they can pull down the house," said Edd.

"Well, we can't have that now, can we? You'll 'ave to get 'im into this room," the ghost said, "coz it's the only one in the house I can haunt."

"No problem," said Edd. "I'll help you spook him out!"

With that, Frank the Ghost seemed happier and disappeared back through the wall.

"SPOOOOOOOOO-KY!!!" thought Edd. "This sounds better than biting legs."

The following day the Councillor turned up late.
Frank was hovering in Edd's room. "Now, remember, if ya can get Mr Council-Pants up 'ere, I'll show him a thing or two."

Edd skipped down the stairs. The Councillor was
waiting alone in the front room. He was a bald man with a
nasty habit of picking his nose. The young duck sneaked
up behind him and stealthily removed the fountain-pen
from his top pocket.

Part one of Edd's plan was complete.

"Is there really nothing I can do?" asked Aunt Vera, joining them.

"Not a sausage," smirked the Councillor, slamming the papers on to the table. He was the nastiest man Edd had ever met.

"You may as well sign without a fuss," he said as he reached in his top pocket. "That's funny! Lost my pen now. Oh come on woman, get a pen and sign!" He was impatient as well as nasty.

Aunt Vera rummaged through the bureau drawers.
"Edd, have you taken all my pens?" she asked.
"No, Auntie!"
"I don't believe it!" The Councillor raised his eyes to
heaven.
"There's loads of pens in my room, but you'll have to get
them yourself, baldie!" Edd said rudely.
The Councillor made a fist. Edd thought he was about
to get walloped, but the Councillor was only looking at his
watch.
"I haven't got all day, you know. Where's this brat's
room? I'll get a pen."
"Show the nice man your room, Edd," commanded Aunt
Vera.
"With pleasure!" said the young duck, smiling.

As the Councillor walked into Edd's room, Frank's ghostly magic began.

Two ballpoints, three pencils and a set of felt-tips started to dance in mid-air. A jet of ink flew across the room and caught the bald man full in the face – SPLAT!

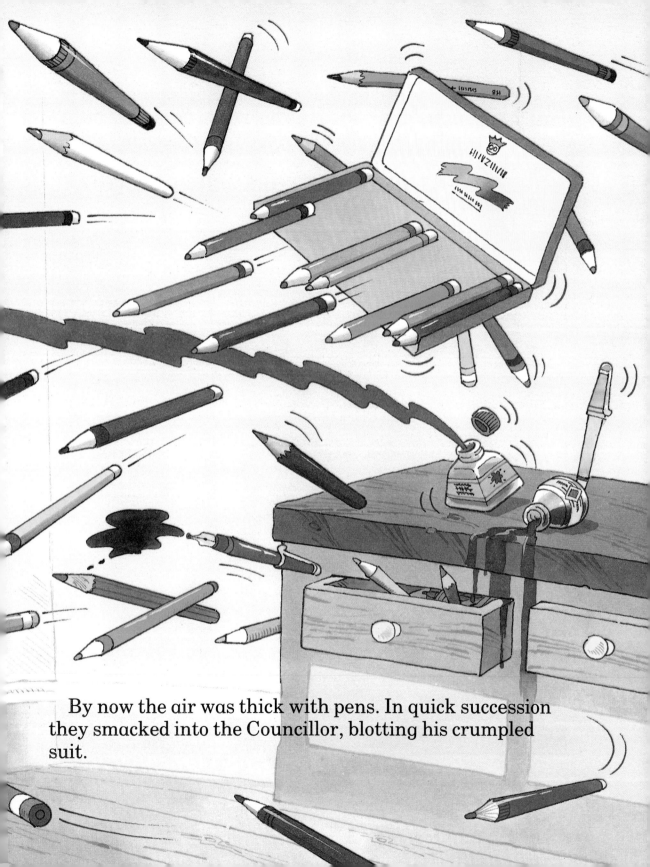

By now the air was thick with pens. In quick succession they smacked into the Councillor, blotting his crumpled suit.

Next Frank decided to undo the bald man's braces. In a flash his trousers dropped to the floor. Edd threw his head back and laughed. His ghostly friend took a deep breath and bellowed,

"GET OUT OF MY HOUSE FOREVER . . . OR YOU WILL BE SORRY!"

The Councillor shrieked and dashed towards the stairs, tripping over his trousers and skidding on the pens.

Bang, bang, bang, CREAK, C-RASH!!!!
"Look at my stairs," cried Aunt Vera, pointing to a splintered hole where the creaking step had been. Before she could say another word, the bald man picked himself up and ran screaming out of the house with the remains of the tenth stair still around his ankle.

Aunt Vera looked very confused.

"It's like he's seen a ghost," she said.

Edd smiled. Suddenly his eye caught sight of something shiny.

"Cor! Treasure!" he exclaimed.

Through the broken stair a metal box was clearly visible. Edd held his breath as Aunt Vera rescued it and lifted the lid.

"It's not treasure," she sighed.

"Not even one diamond?" inquired Edd, crestfallen.

What there was, however, was a large, yellowing document with a big red seal. Aunt Vera unfolded it and began to read. Suddenly she squealed.

"What is it?" Edd was beside himself with curiosity.

"The house . . . the house is saved!" she cried. "Listen to this."

She cleared her throat and read from the document.
"'Whoever lives in Mallard Manor now or at any time in the future is protected by Royal Command. Signed for the King by Lord Mallard, 1637.'"

Frank, who was listening in Edd's room, cartwheeled with joy in the air. All in all, it had been a spookily awesome morning!

A few days later Edd's mum returned to pick him up.

"That's the last bag," said Aunt Vera, pushing the bootlid down. "Tell Edd that he can stay here any time he likes – now that Mallard Manor is to remain in the family. He's . . . er . . . um . . . not such a bad duck most of the time," she admitted.

"Edd! Come on!" Aunt Vera called, looking up at the house. At his bedroom window Edd was standing with a sheet over his head, waving.

"Come on, Edd, stop that," she cried.

"Stop what?" asked Edd quizzically. He'd been standing right next to her all along.

"Well, who's that?" Aunt Vera looked back to the window, but whoever it was had gone.

"A g . . . g . . . ghost!" Aunt Vera stammered. "I thought I saw a ghost."

"Oh, stuff and nonsense!" Edd said, smiling. "That's FRANKLY ridiculous!"

Published by BBC Books,
a division of BBC Enterprises Limited,
Woodlands, 80 Wood Lane, London W12 0TT
First published 1990
Text © Christina Mackay-Robinson 1990
Illustrations © Paul Johnson 1990
ISBN 0 563 36063 1

Set in 9/10 Century Schoolbook by Goodfellow & Egan Ltd, Cambridge
Printed and bound in Great Britain by Cambus Litho Ltd, East Kilbride
Colour separations by Dot Gradations Ltd, Chelmsford
Cover printed by Richard Clay Ltd, Norwich